DOCTOR DOLITTLE

THE BRAVEST MAN IN THE WORLD

DOCTOR DOLITTLE

THE BRAVEST MAN IN THE WORLD

From the stories by
HUGH LOFTING

Abridged by
CHARLIE SHEPPARD

RED FOX

A Red Fox Book

Published by Random House Children's Books
20 Vauxhall Bridge Road, London SW1V 2SA

A division of Random House UK Ltd
London Melbourne Sydney Auckland
Johannesburg and agencies throughout the world

1 3 5 7 9 10 8 6 4 2

This Junior Novel first published in Great Britain
by Red Fox 1999

Printed and bound in Norway by
AIT Trondheim AS

Papers used by Random House UK Limited are natural, recyclable products
made from wood grownin sustainable forests. The manufacturing processes
conform to the environmental regulations of the country of origin.

RANDOM HOUSE UK Limited Reg. No. 954009

ISBN 0 09 940452 4

Contents

1. The Cobbler's Son

First of all I must tell you something about myself. My name is Tommy Stubbins, son of Jacob Stubbins, the cobbler of Puddleby-on-the-Marsh; and I was nine and a half years old when I first met the famous Doctor Dolittle.

At that time Puddleby was only quite a small town. A river ran through the middle of it, and over this river there was a very old stone bridge called Kingsbridge, which led you from the market place on one side to the churchyard on the other.

Sailing ships came up this river from the sea and anchored near the bridge. I used to go down and watch the sailors unloading the ships upon the river wall. The sailors sang strange songs as they pulled upon the ropes, and I learned these songs by heart. I would sit on the river wall with my feet dangling over the water and sing with the men, pretending to myself that I was a sailor.

I longed to sail away with those brave ships when they turned their backs on Puddleby Church and went creeping down the river again, across the wide, lonely marshes to the sea. I longed to go with them out into the world to seek my fortune in foreign lands – Africa, India, China and Peru! When they got round the bend in the river and the water was hidden from view, you could still see their huge brown sails towering over the roofs of the town, moving onward slowly – like some gentle giants that walked among the houses without noise. What strange things would they have seen, I wondered, when they next came back to anchor at Kingsbridge! And dreaming of the lands I had never seen, I'd keep sitting on the river wall, watching till they were out of sight.

I did not go to school, because my father was not rich enough to send me. However, I was

extremely fond of animals, so I used to spend my time collecting birds' eggs and butterflies, fishing in the river, rambling through the countryside after blackberries and mushrooms, and helping the mussel man mend his nets.

Yes, it was a very pleasant life I lived in those days long ago – though of course I did not think so then. I was nine and a half years old, and, like all boys, wanted to grow up – not knowing how well off I was with no cares and nothing to worry me. I longed for the time when I should be allowed to leave home, to travel on one of those brave ships, to sail down the river through the misty marshes to the sea – out into the world to seek my fortune.

One early morning in the springtime, when I was wandering among the hills at the back of the town, I happened to come upon a hawk with a squirrel in its claws. It was standing on a rock and the squirrel was fighting very hard for its life. The hawk was so frightened when I came upon it suddenly like this that it dropped the poor creature and flew away. I picked the squirrel up and found that two of its legs were badly hurt. So I carried it in my arms back to

my bedroom at the top of the house.

Later that afternoon Matthew Mugg, the cat's meat man, came round, and I asked him if he could do anything for the poor squirrel. He put on his spectacles and examined it carefully. Then he shook his head.

'Your squirrel's got a broken leg,' he said. 'This is a job for a surgeon - and a right smart one an' all. There be only one man I know who could save your creature's life. And that's John Dolittle.'

'Who is John Dolittle?' I asked. 'Is he a vet?'

'No,' said Matthew, 'he's no vet. Doctor Dolittle is a naturalist.'

'What's a naturalist?'

'A naturalist,' said Matthew, 'is a person who knows all about animals and butterflies and plants and rocks an' all. John Dolittle is a very great naturalist. I'm surprised you never heard of him – and you daft over animals. He's a great man, a very great man. And as for animals, well, there ain' no one knows as much about 'em as what he does.'

'How did he get to know so much about animals?' I asked.

Matthew leaned down to whisper in my ear. 'He talks their language,' he said in a hoarse mysterious voice.

'The animals' language?' I cried.

'Why certainly,' said Matthew. 'All animals have some kind of a language. Some sorts talk more than others; some only speak in sign language. But the Doctor, he understands them all – birds as well as animals. We keep it a secret though, him and me, because folks only laugh at you when you speak of it. Why he can even write animal language. He reads aloud to his pets. He's wrote history books in monkey talk, poetry in canary language, and comic songs for magpies to sing. It's a fact. He's a great man.'

'He certainly must be,' I said. 'I do wish I could meet him.'

'Well there's his house, look,' said the cat's-meat-man walking to the window. 'That little one at the bend in the road there – the one high up – like it was sitting on the wall above the street.'

The house that Matthew pointed out was quite a small one standing by itself. There seemed to be a big garden around it. This garden was much higher than the road, so you had to go up a flight of steps in the wall before you reached the front gate at the top.

I thanked Matthew Mugg and leaving my poor squirrel in a box filled with straw, I started off towards the Doctor's house. On the way I noticed that the sky was clouding over and that it looked as though it might rain.

2. The Great Doctor Dolittle

I reached the gate and found it locked. I began to fear that my squirrel would die before the Doctor came back. I turned away sadly, went down the steps on to the road and turned towards home again. All of a sudden the rain came down in torrents.

I have never seen it rain so hard. It got dark almost like night. The wind began to blow; the thunder rolled; the lightning flashed; and in a moment the gutters of the road were flowing like a river. There was no place handy to take shelter so I put my head down against the driving wind and started to run towards home.

I hadn't gone very far when my head

bumped into something soft and I sat down suddenly on the pavement. I looked up to see whom I had run into. And there in front of me, sitting on the wet pavement like myself, was a little round man with a very kind face. He wore a shabby high hat and in his hand he had a small black bag.

'I'm very sorry,' I said. 'I had my head down and I didn't see you coming.'

To my great surprise, instead of getting angry at being knocked down, the little man began to laugh.

'You know, this reminds me,' he said, 'of a time once when I was in India. I ran full tilt into a woman in a thunderstorm. But she was carrying a pitcher of treacle on her head and I had sticky hair for weeks afterwards – the flies followed me everywhere. I didn't hurt you, did I?'

'No,' I said. 'I'm all right.'

'It was just as much my fault as it was yours, you know,' said the little man. 'I had my head down too – but look here, we mustn't sit talking like this. You must be soaked. I know I am. How far have you got to go?'

'My home is on the other side of the town,' I said as we picked ourselves up.

'My goodness, but that was a wet pavement!' the little man said. 'And I declare it's coming down worse than ever. Come along to my house and get dried. A storm like this can't last.'

He picked himself up and ran off down the

road. Quick as a flash I decided to go with him. As we ran along together I began to wonder who this funny little man could be, and where he lived. I was a stranger to him, and yet he was kindly taking me to his own home to get dried.

'Here we are,' he said.

I looked up to see where we were and found myself back at the foot of the steps leading to the little house with the big garden! My new friend was already running up the steps and opening the gate with some keys he took from his pocket.

'Surely,' I thought, 'this cannot be the great Doctor Dolittle himself!'

I suppose after hearing so much about him I had expected someone very tall and strong and marvellous. It was hard to believe that this funny little man with the kind smiling face could really be such a great man. Yet here he was, sure enough, running up the steps and opening the gate.

'Are you Doctor Dolittle?' I shouted as we sped up the short garden path to the house.

'Yes, I'm Doctor Dolittle,' he said, opening the front door with the same bunch of keys.

The storm had made it dark enough outside, but inside the house, with the door closed, it was as black as night. Then began the most extraordinary noise that I have ever heard. It sounded like all sorts of animals and birds calling and squeaking and screeching at the same time. I could hear things trundling down the stairs and hurrying along passages.

Somewhere in the dark a duck was quacking, a cock was crowing, a dove was cooing, an owl was hooting, a lamb was bleating, and a dog was barking. I felt birds' wings fluttering and fanning near my face. Things kept bumping into my legs and nearly upsetting me. The whole front hall seemed to be filling up with animals. The noise, together with the roaring of the rain, was tremendous.

I was beginning to grow a little bit scared, but the Doctor took hold of my arm and shouted into my ear, 'Don't be alarmed. Don't be frightened. These are just some of my pets.'

So there I stood in the pitch-black dark, while all kinds of animals, that I couldn't see, chattered and jostled around me. It all seemed like some strange dream and I was beginning to wonder if I was really awake, when I heard the Doctor speaking again. 'My blessed matches are all wet. They won't strike. Have you got any?' he asked.

'No, I'm afraid I haven't,' I called back.

'Never mind,' he said. 'Perhaps Dab-Dab can raise us a light somewhere.'

Then the Doctor made some funny clicking noises with his tongue and I heard someone trundle up the stairs again and start moving about in the rooms above.

Then we waited quite a while without anything happening.

'Will the light be long in coming?' I asked. 'Some animal is sitting on my foot and my toes are going to sleep.'

'No, only a minute,' said the Doctor. 'She'll be back in a minute.'

And just then I saw the first glimmerings of a light around the landing above. At once all the animals kept quiet.

'I thought you lived alone,' I said to the Doctor.

'So I do,' he said. 'It is Dab-Dab who is bringing the light.'

I looked up the stairs, trying to make out who was coming. I could not see around the landing, but I heard the most curious footstep on the upper flight. It sounded like someone hopping down from one step to the other on one leg.

As the light came lower, it grew brighter and began to throw strange shadows on the walls.

'Ah – at last!' said the Doctor. 'Good old Dab–Dab!'

And then I thought I really must be dreaming. For there, craning her neck round the bend of the landing, hopping down the stairs on one leg, came a spotless white duck. And in her right foot she carried a lighted candle!

3. Doctor Dolittle's Home

When at last I could look around me, I found that the hall really was full of animals. It seemed to me that almost every kind of creature from the countryside must be there: a pigeon, a white mouse, an owl, a badger, a jackdaw – there was even a small pig, just in from the rainy garden, carefully wiping his feet on the mat while the light from the candle glistened on his wet pink back.

The Doctor took the candlestick from the duck and turned to me.

'By the way,' he said, 'what is your name?'

'Tommy Stubbins,' I said.

'Oh, are you the son of Jacob Stubbins,

17

the shoemaker?'

'Yes,' I said.

'Excellent bootmaker, your father,' said the Doctor. 'You see these?' and he held up his right foot to show me the enormous boots he was wearing. 'Your father made those boots four years ago, and I've been wearing them ever since – perfectly wonderful boots. Well now, look here, Stubbins. You've got to change those wet things – and quick. Wait a moment till I get some more candles lit, and then we'll go upstairs and find some dry clothes. You'll have to wear an old suit of mine till we can get yours dry again by the kitchen fire.'

We changed into two suits of the Doctor's. Then we carried our wet ones into the kitchen and started a fire in the big chimney. The coat of the Doctor's that I was wearing was so large for me that I kept treading on my own coat-tails while I was helping to fetch the wood up from the cellar. But very soon we had a huge fire blazing up the chimney and we hung our wet clothes around on chairs.

'You'll stay and have supper with me, Stubbins, of course?'

Already I was beginning to feel very fond of this funny little man. He seemed to begin right away treating me as though I were a grown-up friend of his. And when he asked me to stop and have supper with him I felt terribly proud and happy. But I suddenly remembered that I had not told my mother that I would be out late. So very sadly I answered, 'Thank you very much. I would like to stay, but I am afraid that my mother will begin to worry and wonder where I am if I don't get back.'

'Oh, but my dear Stubbins,' said the Doctor, throwing another log of wood on the fire, 'your clothes aren't dry yet. You'll have to wait for them, won't you? By the time they are ready to put on, we will have supper cooked and eaten. Did you see where I put my bag?'

I found the bag near the front door. It was made of black leather and looked very, very old. One of its latches was broken and it was tied up around the middle with a piece of string.

'Thank you,' said the Doctor when I brought it to him, and he started to feel inside it.

First he brought out a loaf of new bread. Next came a glass jar of marmalade which he

set upon the table. At last the Doctor brought
out a pound of sausages.

'Now,' he said, 'all we want is a frying pan.'
We went into the scullery and there we
found some pots and pans hanging against the
wall. The Doctor took down the frying pan and

in a few moments the sausages were sending a beautiful smell all through the room.

'Ah,' said the Doctor. 'The sausages are done to a turn. Come along – hold your plate near and let me give you some.'

Then we sat down at the kitchen table and started a hearty meal. It was a wonderful kitchen, that. I had many meals there afterwards and I found it a better place to eat in than the grandest dining room in the world. It was so cosy and home-like and warm. It was handy for the food too. You took it right off the fire, hot, and put it on the table and ate it. And you could watch your toast toasting and see it didn't burn while you drank your soup. Then the fireplace – the biggest fireplace you ever saw – was like a room in itself. You could get right inside it even when the logs were burning and sit on the wide seats either side and roast chestnuts after the meal was over – or listen to the kettle singing, or tell stories, or look at picture books by the light of the fire. It was a marvellous kitchen. It was like the Doctor, comfortable, sensible, friendly and solid.

'Can you really talk to animals?' I asked

while we were gobbling away.

'Oh, yes,' replied the Doctor.

'Can you talk in squirrel language?' I asked.

'Of course. That's quite an easy language,' said the Doctor. 'You could learn that yourself without a great deal of trouble. But why do you ask?'

'Because I have a sick squirrel at home,' I said. 'I took it away from a hawk. But one of its legs is badly hurt and I would really like you to have a look at it. Shall I bring it tomorrow?'

'Well if its leg is badly broken I think I had better see it tonight. It may be too late to do much, but I'll come home with you and take a look at it.'

So presently we felt the clothes by the fire and mine were quite dry. I took them upstairs to the bedroom and changed, and when I came down the Doctor was all ready waiting for me with his little black bag full of medicines and bandages.

'Come along,' he said. 'The rain has stopped now.'

Outside it had grown bright again and the evening sky was all red with the setting sun; and

the thrushes were singing in the garden as we
opened the gate to go down on to the road.

4. Polynesia and the Squirrel

'I think your house is the most interesting house I was ever in,' I said as we set off in the direction of the town. 'May I come and see you again tomorrow?'

'Certainly,' said the Doctor. 'Come any day you like.'

'It must be fantastic,' I said, as we set off in the direction of my home, 'to be able to talk all the languages of the different animals. Do you think I could ever learn to do it?'

'Oh, certainly,' said the Doctor, 'with practice. You have to be very patient, you know. You really ought to have Polynesia to start you. It was she who gave me my first lessons.'

'Who is Polynesia?' I asked.

'Polynesia is a West African parrot. Good old Polynesia. A most extraordinary bird. Here she comes . . .'

A grey and scarlet parrot was skimming down the lane towards us. She flew straight on to the Doctor's shoulder, where she immediately began talking in a language I could not understand. And very soon the Doctor had forgotten all about me and my squirrel and everything else, till at last the bird clearly asked him something about me.

'Oh, excuse me, Stubbins!' said the Doctor. 'I was so interested listening to my old friend here. We must get on and see this squirrel of yours. Polynesia, this is Thomas Stubbins.'

The parrot, on the Doctor's shoulder, nodded gravely towards me and then, to my great surprise, said quite plainly in English, 'How do you do? I remember the night you were born. It was a terribly cold winter. You were a very ugly baby.'

'Stubbins is anxious to learn animal language,' said the Doctor. 'I was just telling him about you and the lessons you gave me.'

'Well,' said the parrot, turning to me, 'I may have started the Doctor learning but I never could have done even that if he hadn't first taught me to understand what I was saying when I spoke English. You see, many parrots can talk like a person, but very few of them understand what they are saying. They just say it because – well, because they fancy it is smart or because they know they will get crackers given to them.'

By this time we had turned and were going towards my home with Polynesia still perched on the Doctor's shoulder. When we arrived at my home, my mother was standing at the door looking down the street.

'Good evening, Mrs Stubbins,' said the Doctor. 'It is my fault your son is so late. I made him stay to supper while his clothes were drying. He was soaked to the skin and so was I. We ran into one another in the storm and I insisted on his coming into my house for shelter.'

'I was beginning to get worried about him,' said my mother. 'I am thankful to you, sir, for looking after him so well and bringing him home.'

'Don't mention it – don't mention it,' said the Doctor. 'We have had a very interesting chat.'

'Who might it be that I have the honour of addressing?' asked my mother, staring at the grey and scarlet parrot perched on the Doctor's shoulder.

'Oh, I'm John Dolittle.'

'The Doctor has come to cure my squirrel, Mother,' I said. 'He knows all about animals.'

'Oh, no,' said the Doctor, 'not all, Stubbins, not all about them by any means.'

'It is very kind of you to come so far to look after his pet,' said my mother. 'Tom is always bringing home strange creatures from the woods and the fields.'

'Is he?' said the Doctor. 'Perhaps he will grow up to be a naturalist some day. Who knows?'

Then I led the Doctor to my bedroom at the top of the house and showed him the squirrel in the box filled with straw.

The animal, who had seemed very much afraid of me – though I had tried to make him feel at home – sat up at once when the Doctor came into the room and started to chatter. The

Doctor chattered back in the same way and the squirrel, when he was lifted up to have his leg examined, appeared to be pleased rather than frightened.

HUGH LOFTING

I held a candle while the doctor tied the leg up in what he called 'splints', which he made out of matchsticks with his penknife.

'I think you will find that his leg will get better now in a very short time,' said the Doctor closing up his bag. 'Don't let him run about for at least two weeks yet, but keep him in the open air and cover him up with dry leaves if the nights get cool. He tells me he is rather lonely here, all by himself, and is wondering how his wife and children are getting on. I have assured him you are a man to be trusted, and I will send a squirrel who lives in my garden to find out how his family are and to bring him news of them. He must be kept cheerful at all costs. Squirrels are naturally a very cheerful, active race. It is very hard for them to lie still doing nothing. But you needn't worry about him. He will be all right.'

5. Polynesia has a Plan

The next morning, I was up very early. I could hardly wait to get back to see the Doctor and his animal family. For the first time in my life I forgot all about breakfast, and creeping down the stairs on tiptoe, so as not to wake my mother and father, I opened the front door and popped out into the empty, silent street.

When I got to the Doctor's house I looked into the garden. No one seemed to be about. So I opened the gate quietly and went inside.

As I turned to go down the path, I heard a voice quite close to me say, 'Good morning. How early you are!'

I turned around, and there, sitting on the top

of a privet hedge, was the grey and scarlet parrot, Polynesia.

'Good morning,' I said. 'I suppose I am rather early. Is the Doctor still in bed?'

'Oh, no,' said Polynesia. 'He has been up an hour and a half. You'll find him in the house somewhere. The front door is open. Just push it and go in. He is sure to be in the kitchen cooking breakfast – or working in his study. Walk right in.'

'Thank you,' I said. I'll go and look for him.'

When I opened the front door I could smell bacon frying. So I made my way to the kitchen.

'Good morning, Stubbins,' said Doctor Dolittle. 'Have you had your breakfast yet?'

I told the Doctor that I had forgotten all about it, so he passed the rack of toast towards me and said, 'Sit down and join me. Have some bacon.'

That was the second time I had seen the Doctor and it was the second time we had eaten together. From then on, and for many years to come, I was to sit at the Doctor's table in Puddleby – and in many strange places all over the world.

Just at that moment, Polynesia came into the room and said something to the Doctor in bird language. Of course I did not understand what it was. But the Doctor at once put down his knife and fork and left the room.

'You know, it is an awful shame,' said the parrot as soon as the Doctor had closed the door. 'All the animals over the whole countryside get to hear of him and every sick cat and mangy rabbit for miles around comes to see him and ask his advice. The animals are so inconsiderate at times – especially the mothers. They come round and call the Doctor away from his meals and wake him out of his bed at all hours of the night. I don't know how he stands it – really I don't.'

'Do you think I would ever be able to learn the language of the animals?' I asked, laying the doctor's plate upon the hearth.

'Well, it all depends,' said Polynesia. 'Are you a good noticer? I mean, for instance, supposing you saw two cock-starlings on an apple tree, and you only took one good look at them – would you be able to tell one from the other if you saw them again the next day?'

33

'I don't know,' I said. 'I've never tried.'

'Well that is what you call powers of observation – noticing the small things about birds and animals: the way they walk and move their heads and flip their wings; the way they sniff the air and twitch their whiskers and wiggle their tails. You have to notice all those little things if you want to learn animal language. That is the first thing to remember: being a good noticer is terribly important in learning animal language.'

'It sounds pretty hard,' I said.

'You'll have to be very patient,' said Polynesia. 'It takes a long time to say even a few words properly. But if you come here often I'll give you a few lessons myself. And once you get started you'll be surprised how fast you get on. It would be a very good thing indeed if you could learn, because then you could do some of the work for the Doctor – I mean the easier work, like bandaging and giving pills. Yes, yes, that's a good idea of mine. 'Twould be a great thing if the poor man could get some help – and some rest. It is a scandal the way he works. I see no reason why you shouldn't be able to help him a great deal. That is, if you are really interested in animals.'

'Oh, I'd love that!' I cried. 'Do you think the Doctor would let me?'

'Certainly,' said Polynesia, 'as soon as you have learned something about doctoring. I'll speak to him about it myself.'

6. My Lessons Begin

Well, there were not many days after that
when I did not come to see my friend.
Indeed I was at his house practically all day and
every day. So that one evening my mother asked
me jokingly why I did not take my bed over
there and live at the Doctor's house altogether.

I met all the Doctor's animal friends, for
besides Dab-Dab and Polynesia there were many
other animal residents at the Doctor's house.
John Dolittle was particularly fond of Gub-Gub
the pig, Chee-Chee the monkey, Too-Too the
clever owl and Jip the loyal dog. Many an
evening we would all sit around the fire and the
Doctor would tell me of the wonderful voyages
and adventures he had undertaken.

After a while I think I got to be quite useful
to the Doctor, feeding his pets for him; helping
with the sick animals that came; doing odd jobs
about the place. So that although I enjoyed it all
very much, I really think the Doctor would
have missed me if I had not come so often.

And all that time, Polynesia came with me
wherever I went, teaching me bird language and
showing me how to understand the talking signs
of the animals. Oh, I was slow at first and
Polynesia often scolded me for not remembering
something that she had told me over and over.

But gradually I could interpret all the wigglings of tails and twitching of noses and squeaks and squawks that formed the animals' messages to humans.

One day Polynesia and I were talking in the library.

'Polynesia,' I said, 'I want to ask you something very important.'

'What is it, my boy?' she said, smoothing down the feathers of her right wing.

'Listen,' I said, 'my mother doesn't think it is right that I come here for so many meals. And I was going to ask you: supposing I did a whole lot more work for the Doctor – why couldn't I come and live here altogether? You see, instead of being paid like a regular workman, I would get my bed and meals in exchange for the work I did. What do you think?'

'You mean you want to be a proper assistant to the Doctor, is that it?' she asked.

'Yes, I suppose that's what you'd call it,' I answered. 'You know you said yourself that you thought I could be very useful to him.'

'Humph – let's go and speak to the Doctor about it,' said Polynesia. 'He's in the study. Open the door very gently – he may be working and not want to be disturbed.'

Presently the Doctor looked up and saw us at the door.

'Oh – come in, Stubbins,' he said. 'Did you wish to speak to me? Come in and take a chair.'

'Doctor,' I said, 'I want to be a naturalist – like you – when I grow up.'

'Oh, you do, do you?' murmured the Doctor. 'Humph – well! Dear me! You don't say! Well, well! Have you, er – have you spoken to your mother and father about it?'

'No, not yet,' I said. 'I want you to speak to them for me. You would do it better. I want to be your assistant, if you'll have me. My mother doesn't think it's right for me to come here so often for meals. And I've been thinking about it a good deal since. Couldn't we make some arrangement – couldn't I work for my meals and sleep here?'

'But my dear Stubbins,' said the Doctor, laughing, 'you are quite welcome to come here for three meals a day all year round. I'm only too glad to have you. Besides, you do do a lot of work as it is. But what arrangement was it that you thought of?' asked the Doctor.

'Well, I thought,' I said, 'that perhaps you would come and see my mother and father and tell them that if they let me live here with you and work hard, you will teach me to read and write. You see my mother is awfully anxious to have me learn reading and writing. Besides, if I'm living with you, and sort of belong to your house and business, I shall be able to come with you next time you go on a voyage.'

'Oh, I see,' he said, smiling. 'So you want to come on a voyage with me, do you? Aha!'

'I want to go on all your voyages with you. It would be much easier for you if you had someone to carry the butterfly-nets and notebooks. Wouldn't it now?'

For a long time the Doctor sat thinking, drumming the desk with his fingers, while I waited, terribly impatiently, to see what he was going to say.

At last he shrugged his shoulders and stood up.

'Well Stubbins,' he said, 'I'll come and talk it over with you and your parents – say – next Thursday. And – well, we'll see. We'll see.'

Then I tore home to tell my mother and father that the Doctor was coming to see them next Thursday.

7. Doctor Dolittle's Assistant

When Thursday evening came, there was great excitement at our house. My mother had asked me what the Doctor's favourite dishes were, and I had told her: spare ribs, sliced beetroot, fried bread, shrimps, and treacle tart. Tonight she had them all on the table waiting for him, and she was now fussing round the house to see if everything was tidy and ready for his visit.

At last we heard a knock on the door, and of course it was I who rushed to be the first to let him in.

'Good evening, Stubbins,' he laughed, handing me his hat.

After supper was over (which he enjoyed
very much), the table was cleared away and the
washing-up left in the kitchen sink till the next
day. Then the Doctor and my mother and father
began talking about my future.

'Your son tells me that he is anxious to be a
naturalist,' said the Doctor.

And then began a long talk which lasted far

into the night. At first my mother and father were rather against the idea. They said it was only a boyish whim and that I would get tired of it very soon. But after the matter had been talked over from every side, the Doctor turned to my father and said, 'Well now, supposing, Mr Stubbins, that your son came to me for two years – that is, until he is twelve years old. During those two years he will have time to see if he is going to grow tired of it or not. Also, during that time, I will promise to teach him reading and writing and perhaps a little arithmetic as well.'

Then my mother spoke up. She pointed out to my father that this was a grand chance for me to get some education. 'Tommy can easily spare these two years for his education; and if he learns no more than to read and write, the time will not be have been lost.'

Well, at length my father gave in; and it was agreed that I was to go to live at the Doctor's house for the next two years.

There surely was never a happier boy in the world than I was at that moment. At last the dream of my life was to come true! At last I was to be given a chance to seek my fortune, to have adventure! For I knew perfectly well that it was now almost time for the Doctor to start upon another voyage. Polynesia had told me that he hardly ever stayed home for more than six months at a stretch. Therefore he would surely be going again within a fortnight. And I – I, Tommy Stubbins, would go with him. Just to think of it! To cross the sea, to walk on foreign shores, to roam the world!

8. Blind Travel

The next day I moved to the Doctor's house and from then on – and for many years after – my time was filled with study and happy companionship with all the animals of the household as I learned more and more to speak their language.

After two weeks I became desperate to go on a voyage so I asked the Doctor if we would be going away soon. He looked up sharply and I suppose he saw how anxious I was because he suddenly smiled his old, boyish smile and said, 'Yes, Stubbins. Don't worry. We'll go. I mustn't stop exploring and learning. But where to go? That's the question. Where shall we go?'

There were so many places that I wanted to go that I couldn't make up my mind right away. And while I was still thinking, the Doctor sat up in his chair and said, 'I'll tell you what we'll do, Stubbins: it's a game I used to play when I was young. I used to call it Blind Travel. Whenever I wanted to go on a voyage and couldn't make up my mind where to go, I would take the atlas and open it with my eyes shut. Next, I'd wave a pencil, still without looking, and stick it down on whatever page had fallen open. Then I'd open my eyes and look. It's a very exciting game, is Blind Travel. Because you have to swear before you begin that you will go to the place the pencil touches, come what may. Shall we play it?'

'Oh, let's!' I almost yelled. 'How thrilling! I hope it's China . . . or Borneo . . . or Baghdad.'

And in a moment I had scrambled up the bookcase, dragged the big atlas from the top shelf and laid it on the table before the Doctor.

I knew every page in that atlas by heart. How many days and nights I had lingered over its faded maps, following the blue rivers from the mountains to the sea, wondering what the

little towns really looked like and how wide
were the sprawling lakes!

As the Doctor began sharpening his pencil, a
thought came to me.

'What if the pencil falls upon the North
Pole?' I asked. 'Will we have to go there?'

'No, the rules of the game say you don't have

to go to any place you've been to before. You are allowed another try. I've been to the North Pole,' he ended quietly, 'so we shan't have to go there.'

I could hardly speak with astonishment. 'You've been to the North Pole!' I managed to gasp out at last. 'But I thought it was still undiscovered. The map shows all the places explorers have reached trying to get there. Why isn't your name down if you discovered it?'

'I promised to keep it a secret. And you must promise me never to tell anyone. Yes, I discovered the North Pole in April, 1809. But shortly after I got there the polar bears came to me and told me there was a great deal of coal there, buried beneath the snow. They knew, they said, that human beings would do anything and go anywhere to get coal. So would I please keep it a secret. So of course I had to promise them I would. Ah, well, it will be discovered again some day, by somebody else. But I want the polar bears to have their playground to themselves for as long as possible. And I daresay it will be a good while yet, for it certainly is a fiendish place to get to. Well, now, are we ready? Good! Take the pencil and stand here close to the table. When the book falls open, wave the pencil around three times and jab it down. Ready? All right, shut your eyes.'

HUGH LOFTING

It was a tense and fearful moment – but very thrilling. We both had our eyes shut tight. I heard the atlas fall open with a bang. I wondered which page it was showing. So much would depend on where that pencil landed. I waved three times in a circle. I began to lower my hand. The pencil point touched the page and my voyages with Doctor Dolittle were about to begin . . .

We both opened our eyes, then bumped our heads together with a crack in our eagerness to lean over and see where we were to go.

The atlas lay open and my pencil point was resting right in the centre of a group of islands. The name of them was printed so small that the Doctor had to get out his strong spectacles to read it. I was trembling with excitement.

'Capa Blanca Islands,' he read out slowly.

'We'll go there, Doctor, won't we?' I asked.

'Of course we will. The rules of the game say we've got to.'

'It'll be a grand voyage. Look at the sea we've got to cross.'

How like a dream it all sounded! The two of us sitting there at the big study table, the candles lit, the smoke curling towards the dim ceiling from the Doctor's pipe. I could contain myself no longer. I was bursting to tell someone. I ran dancing and singing from the room to find Polynesia.

At the door I tripped over Dab-Dab, who was just coming in with her wings full of plates, and fell headlong on my nose.

HUGH LOFTING

'Has the boy gone crazy?' cried the duck. 'Where do you think you're going?'

'To the Capa Blanca Islands!' I shouted, picking myself up and doing cartwheels down the hall. 'The Capa Blanca Islands! Hooray!

'You're going to the madhouse, I should say,' snorted the housekeeper. 'Look what you've done to my best china!'

But I was far too happy to listen to her scolding, and I ran on, singing into the kitchen to find Polynesia.

9. Good-bye!

That same week we began our preparations for the voyage. The mussel man had agreed to lend us a ship and he tied it up along the river wall so it would be handier for loading. And for three whole days we carried provisions down to our beautiful new boat and stowed them away.

I was surprised to find how big the boat was inside. There were three little cabins, a dining room, and underneath all this, a big place called the hold, where the food and extra sails and other things were kept.

Soon we had everything in readiness for our departure. Jip the dog begged so hard to be taken that the Doctor finally gave in and said he could come. Polynesia and Chee-Chee the monkey were the only other animals to go with us. Dab-Dab was left in charge of the house and the rest of the animal family we were leaving behind.

Of course, as is always the way, at the last moment we kept remembering things we had forgotten, and when we finally closed the house up and went down the steps to the street, we were all burdened with armfuls of odd packages.

Down at the river wall we found a great crowd waiting to see us off. Standing right near the gangplank were my mother and father. I hoped that they would not make a scene or burst into tears, or anything like that. But as a matter of fact they behaved quite well – for parents. My mother said something about being sure not to get my feet wet; and my father just smiled a crooked sort of smile, patted me on the back, and wished me luck.

At last, after much pulling and tugging, we got the anchor up and undid a lot of mooring ropes. Soon we were moving gently down the river while the people on the wall cheered and waved their handkerchiefs.

For me indeed it was a great and wonderful feeling, that getting out into the open sea, when at length we passed the little lighthouse at the mouth of the river and found ourselves free of land. It was all so new and different; just the sky above you and sea below. This ship, which was to be our home for so many days to come, seemed so tiny in all this wide water – so tiny and yet so snug and safe.

I looked around me and took a deep breath. The doctor was at the wheel steering the boat which was now leaping and plunging through the waves. Chee-Chee was coiling up ropes in the stern and laying them in neat piles. My work was fastening down the things on the deck so that nothing could roll about if the weather grew rough. Jip was up in the prow of the boat with his ears cocked and his nose stuck out, his keen old eyes keeping a sharp lookout for floating wrecks and other dangers. Each one of us had some special job to do, part of the proper running of a ship. Even old Polynesia was taking the sea's temperature with the Doctor's bath thermometer tied on the end of a string, to make sure there were no icebergs near us. As I

listened to her swearing softly to herself because
she couldn't read the figures in the fading light,
I realized that the voyage had really started and
that very soon it would be night – my first night
at sea!

10. The Capa Blanca Islands

I shall now tell you about the adventure we had when we reached our destination.

Many years ago the Doctor gave me permission to do this. But we were both of us so busy then voyaging around the world, having adventures and filling notebooks full of natural history that I never seemed to get time to sit down and write of our doings.

Now, of course, when I am quite an old man, my memory isn't so good any more. But whenever I am in doubt and have to hesitate and think, I always ask Polynesia, the parrot.

That wonderful bird sits on the top of my desk, usually humming sailor songs to herself while I write this book. And, as everyone who has ever met her knows, Polynesia's memory is the most marvellous memory in the world.

Having been at sea for many days, one Friday morning Polynesia shouted, 'Land Ahoy!' To my amazement I saw some beautiful islands glittering in the distance. We had arrived safely at the Capa Blanca Islands. When we reached these wonderful Spanish islands, we moored the ship and set off to explore.

There was a very funny little town on one island, quite different from any that I had ever seen. The streets were all twisty and winding and so narrow that a wagon could only just pass along them. The houses overhung at the top and came so close together that people in the attics could lean out of the windows and shake hands with their neighbours on the opposite side of the street. The Doctor told us the town was very, very old. It was called Monteverde.

We couldn't afford to go to a hotel or anything like that. But on the second evening when we were passing by a bed maker's shop we noticed several beds, which the man had made, standing

on the pavement outside. The Doctor started
chatting in Spanish to the bed maker, who was
sitting at his door whistling to a parrot in a cage.

The Doctor and the bed maker got very friendly talking about birds and things. And as it grew near to supper-time the man asked us to stop and eat with him.

This of course we were very glad to do. And after the meal was over (very nice dishes they were, mostly cooked in olive oil – I particularly liked the fried bananas), we sat outside on the pavement again and went on talking far into the night.

At last when we got up to go back to our ship, this very nice shopkeeper wouldn't hear of our going away on any account. He said the streets down by the harbour were very badly lit and there was no moon. We would surely get lost. He invited us to spend the night with him and go back to our ship in the morning.

Well, we finally agreed; and as our new friend had no spare bedrooms, the Doctor and I slept on the beds set out for sale on the pavement in front of the shop. The night was so hot we needed no coverings. It was great fun to fall asleep out-of-doors like this, watching the people walking to and fro and the merry life of the streets.

It seemed to me that Spanish people never went to bed at all. Late as it was, all the little restaurants and cafés around us were wide open, with customers drinking coffee and chatting merrily at the small tables outside. The sound of a guitar strumming softly in the distance mingled with the clatter of chinaware and the babble of voices.

Somehow it made me think of my mother and father far away in Puddleby, with their regular habits, the evening practice on the flute and the rest – doing the same thing every day. I felt sort of sorry for them, in a way, because they missed the fun of this travelling life, where we were doing something new all the time – even sleeping differently. But I suppose if they had been invited to go to bed on a pavement in front of a shop they wouldn't have cared for the idea at all. It is funny how some people are.

11. The Doctor's Challenge

Next morning we were awakened by a great racket. There was a procession coming down the street, a number of men in very colourful clothes followed by a large crowd of admiring ladies and cheering children. I asked the Doctor who they were.

'They are the bullfighters,' he said. 'There is to be a bullfight tomorrow.'

'What is a bullfight?' I asked.

To my great surprise, the Doctor got red in the face with anger. It reminded me of the time when he had spoken of wild animals held against their will in zoos.

'A bullfight is a stupid, cruel, disgusting

business,' he said. 'These Spanish people are most loveable and hospitable folk. How they can enjoy these wretched bullfights is a thing I could never understand.'

Then the Doctor went on to explain to me how a bull was first made very angry by teasing and then allowed to run into a circus where men came out with red cloaks, waved them at him, and ran away. Next the bull was allowed to tire himself out by tossing and killing a lot of poor old broken-down horses who couldn't defend themselves. Then, when the bull was thoroughly out of breath and wearied by this, a man came out with a sword and killed the bull.

'Every Sunday,' said the Doctor, 'in almost every big town in Spain, there are six bulls killed like that and as many horses.'

'But aren't the men ever killed by the bull?' I asked.

'Unfortunately very seldom,' he said. 'A bull is not nearly as dangerous as he looks, even when he's angry, if only you are quick on your feet and don't lose your head. These bullfighters are very clever and nimble. And the people, especially the Spanish ladies, think no end of them. A famous bullfighter (or matador, as they call them) is a more important man in Spain than a king - here comes another crowd of them round the corner, look. See the girls throwing kisses to them. Ridiculous business!'

At that moment our friend the bed maker came out to see the procession go past. And while he was wishing us a good morning and inquiring how we slept, a friend of his walked up and joined us. The bed maker introduced this friend to us as Don Enrique Cardenas.

Don Enrique, when he heard where we were from, spoke to us in English. He appeared to be a well-educated, gentlemanly sort of person.

'And you go to see the bullfight tomorrow, yes?' he asked the Doctor pleasantly.

'Certainly not,' said John Dolittle firmly. 'I don't like bullfights – cruel cowardly shows.'

Don Enrique nearly exploded. I never saw a man get so excited. He told the Doctor that he didn't know what he was talking about. He said bullfighting was a noble sport and that the matadors were the bravest men in the world.

'Oh, rubbish!' said the Doctor. 'You never give the poor bull a chance. It is only when he is all tired and dazed that your precious matadors dare to try and kill him.'

I thought the Spaniard was going to hit the Doctor, he got so angry. While he was still spluttering to find words, the bed maker came between them and took the Doctor aside. He explained to John Dolittle, in a whisper, that this Don Enrique Cardenas was a very important person, that he was the man who supplied the bulls – a special, strong black kind – from his own farm for all the bullfights in the Capa Blancas. He was a very rich man, the bed maker said, a most important person. He mustn't be allowed to take offence on any account.

I watched the Doctor's face as the bed maker finished, and I saw a flash of boyish mischief come into his eyes as though an idea had struck him. He turned to the angry Spaniard.

'Don Enrique,' he said, 'you tell me your bullfighters are very brave men and skilful. It seems I have offended you by saying that bullfighting is a poor sport. What is the name of the best matador for tomorrow's show?'

'Pepito de Malaga,' said Don Enrique. 'One of the greatest names, one of the bravest men in all Spain.'

'Very well,' said the Doctor, 'I have a proposal to make to you. I have never fought a bull in my life. Now supposing I were to go into the ring tomorrow with Pepito de Malaga and any other matadors you choose, and if I can do more tricks with a bull than they can, would you promise to do something for me?'

Don Enrique threw back his head and laughed. 'Man,' he said, 'you must be mad! You would be killed at once. One has to be trained for years to become a proper bullfighter.'

'Supposing I were willing to take the risk of that. You are not afraid, I take it, to accept my offer?'

The Spaniard frowned. 'Afraid!' he cried. 'Sir, if you can beat Pepito de Malaga in the bullring, I'll promise you anything it is possible for me to grant.'

'Very good,' said the Doctor. 'Now I understand that you are quite a powerful man in these islands. If you wished to stop all bullfighting here after tomorrow, you could do it, couldn't you?'

'Yes,' said Don Enrique proudly, 'I could.'

'Well, that is what I ask of you – if I win my wager,' said John Dolittle. 'If I can do more with angry bulls than Pepito de Malaga can, you are to promise me that there shall never be another bullfight in the Capa Blancas so long as you are alive to stop it. Is it a deal?'

The Spaniard held out his hand. 'It is a deal,' he said. 'I promise. But I must warn you that you are merely throwing your life away, for you will certainly be killed. However, that is no more than you deserve for saying that bullfighting is an unworthy sport. I will meet you here tomorrow morning if you should wish to arrange any particulars. Good day, sir.'

As the Spaniard turned and walked into the shop with the bed maker, Polynesia, who had been listening as usual, flew up on to my shoulder and whispered in my ear, 'I have a plan. Get hold of Chee-Chee and come some place where the Doctor can't hear us. I want to talk to you.'

I nudged Chee-Chee and we crossed the street and pretended to look into a jeweller's window while the Doctor sat down on his bed to lace up his boots, the only part of his clothing he had taken off for the night.

'Listen,' said Polynesia, 'I've been breaking my head trying to think up some way we can get money to buy more stores with, and at last I've got it.'

'The money?' I said.

'No, the idea – to make the money with. Listen, the Doctor is simply bound to win this game tomorrow, sure as you're alive. Now all we have to do is to make a side bet with these Spaniards and the trick's done.'

'What's a side bet?' Chee-Chee asked.

'Oh, I know what that is,' I said. 'I go to Don Enrique and say, "I bet you a hundred pounds the Doctor wins." Then if he does win, Don Enrique pays me a hundred pounds; and if he doesn't, I have to pay Don Enrique.'

'That's the idea,' said Polynesia. 'Only don't say a hundred pounds – say two thousand five hundred pesetas. Now, come and find old Don Ricky-ticky and try to look rich.'

So we crossed the street again and slipped into the bed maker's shop while the Doctor was still busy with his boots.

'Don Enrique,' I said, standing as tall as I

could, 'allow me to introduce myself. I am Tommy Stubbins of Puddleby-on-the-Marsh, and assistant to Doctor Dolittle. Would you care to have a small bet with me on tomorrow's bullfight?'

Don Enrique bowed.

'Why certainly,' he said, 'I shall be delighted. But I must warn you that you are bound to lose. How much?'

'Oh a mere trifle,' I said. 'Just for the fun of the thing, you know. What do you say to three thousand pesetas?'

'I agree,' said the Spaniard, bowing once more. 'I will meet you after the bullfight tomorrow.'

'So that's all right,' said Polynesia as we came out to join the Doctor. 'I feel as though quite a load has been taken off my mind.'

12. The Great Bullfight

The next day was a great day in Monteverde. All the streets were hung with flags, and everywhere brightly dressed crowds were to be seen flocking towards the bullring – as the big circus was called where the fights took place.

The news of the Doctor's challenge had gone round the town and, it seemed, had caused much amusement to the islanders. The very idea of a mere foreigner daring to match himself against the great Pepito de Malaga! Serve him right if he got killed!

The Doctor had borrowed a bullfighter's suit from Don Enrique; and very merry and wonderful he looked in it, though I had hard work getting the waistcoat to close in front and, even then, the buttons kept bursting off it in all directions.

When we set out from the harbour to walk to the bullring, crowds of small boys ran after us making fun of the Doctor's fatness, calling out, 'Juan Hagapoco, el grueso matador!' which is Spanish for 'John Dolittle, the fat bullfighter.'

As soon as we arrived, the Doctor said he would like to take a look at the bulls before the fight began, and we were at once led to the bull pen where, behind a high railing, six enormous black bulls were tramping round wildly.

In a few hurried words and signs, the Doctor told the bulls what he was going to do and gave them careful instructions for their part of the show. The poor creatures were tremendously glad when they heard that there was a chance of bullfighting being stopped, and they promised to do exactly as they were told.

Of course the man who took us in there didn't understand what we were doing. He merely thought the fat Englishman was crazy when he saw the doctor making signs and talking in ox tongue.

From there the Doctor went to the matadors' dressing rooms while Chee-Chee and I, with Polynesia, made our way into the bullring and took our seats in the great open-air theatre.

It was a very gay sight. Thousands of ladies and gentlemen were there, all dressed in their smartest clothes, and everybody seemed very happy and cheerful.

Right at the beginning Don Enrique got up and explained to the people that the first item on the programme was to be a match between the English Doctor and Pepito de Malaga. He told them what he had promised if the Doctor should win. But the people did not seem to think there was much chance of that. A roar of laughter went up at the very mention of such a thing.

When Pepito came into the ring everybody cheered, the ladies blew kisses, and the men clapped and waved their hats.

Presently a large door on the other side of the ring was rolled back and in galloped one of the bulls; then the door was closed again. At once the matador became very much on the alert. He waved his red cloak and the bull rushed at him. Pepito stepped nimbly aside and the people cheered again.

This game was repeated several times. But I noticed that whenever Pepito got into a tight place and seemed to be in real danger from the bull, an assistant of his, who always hung around somewhere near, drew the bull's attention upon himself by waving another red cloak. Then the bull would chase the assistant and Pepito was left in safety. Most often, as soon as he had drawn the bull off, this assistant ran for the high fence and vaulted out of the ring to save himself. They evidently had it all arranged, these matadors, and it didn't seem to me that they were in any very great danger from the poor clumsy bull so long as they didn't slip and fall.

After about ten minutes of this kind of thing, the small door into the matadors' dressing room opened and the Doctor strolled into the ring. As soon as his fat figure, dressed in sky-blue velvet, appeared, the crowd rocked in their seats with laughter.

Juan Hagapoco, as they had called him, walked out into the centre of the ring and bowed ceremoniously to the ladies in the boxes.

74

Then he bowed to the bull. Then he bowed to Pepito. While he was bowing to Pepito's assistant, the bull started to rush at him from behind.

'Look out! Look out! The bull! You will be killed!' yelled the crowd.

But the Doctor calmly finished his bow. Then turning round he folded his arms, fixed the charging bull with his eye and frowned a terrible frown.

Presently a curious thing happened: the bull's speed got slower and slower. It almost looked as though he were afraid of that frown. Soon he stopped altogether. The Doctor shook his finger at him. He began to tremble. At last, tucking his tail between his legs, the bull turned round and ran away.

The crowd gasped. The Doctor ran after him. Round and round the ring they went, both of them puffing and blowing like grampuses. Excited whispers began to break out among the people. This was something new in bullfighting, to have the bull running away from the man instead of the man away from the bull. At last in the tenth lap, with a final burst of speed, Juan Hagapoco, the English matador, caught the poor bull by the tail.

Then leading the now timid creature into the middle of the ring, the Doctor made him do all manner of tricks: standing on the hind legs, standing on the front legs, dancing, hopping, rolling over. He finished up by making the bull kneel down; then he got on to his back and did handsprings and other acrobatics on the beast's horns.

Pepito and his assistant had their noses sadly out of joint. The crowd had forgotten them entirely. They were standing together by the fence not far from where I sat, muttering to one another and slowly growing green with jealousy.

Finally the Doctor turned towards Don Enrique's seat and bowing said in a loud voice, 'This bull is no good any more. He's terrified and out of breath. Take him away, please.'

'Does the caballero wish for a fresh bull?' asked Don Enrique.

'No,' said the Doctor. 'I want five fresh bulls. And I would like them all in the ring at once please.'

At this, a cry of horror burst from the people. They had been used to seeing matadors escaping from one bull at a time, but five! That must mean certain death.

Pepito sprang forward and called to Don Enrique not to allow it, saying it was against all the rules of bullfighting. ('Ha!' Polynesia chuckled into my ear. 'It's like the Doctor's navigation: he breaks all the rules, but he gets there. If they'll only let him, he'll give them the best show for their money they ever saw.') A great argument began. Half the people seemed to be on Pepito's side and half on the Doctor's side. At last the Doctor turned to Pepito and made another very grand bow which burst the last button off his waistcoat.

'Well, of course if the caballero is afraid . . .' he began with a bland smile.

'Afraid!' screamed Pepito. 'I am afraid of nothing on earth. I am the greatest matador in Spain. With this right hand I have killed nine hundred and fifty-seven bulls.'

'All right then,' said the Doctor, 'let us see if you can kill five more. Let the bulls in!' he shouted. 'Pepito de Malaga is not afraid.'

A dreadful silence hung over the great theatre as the heavy door in the bull pen was rolled back. Then with a roar, the five big bulls bounded into the ring.

'Look fierce,' I heard the Doctor call to them in cattle language. 'Don't scatter. Keep close. Get ready for a rush. Take Pepito, the one in purple, first. But for heaven's sake don't kill him. Just chase him out of the ring. Now then, all together, go for him!'

The bulls put down their heads and all in

78

line, like a squadron of cavalry, charged across the ring straight for poor Pepito.

For one moment the Spaniard tried his hardest to look brave. But the sight of the five pairs of horns coming at him at full gallop was too much. He turned white to the lips, ran for the fence, vaulted it, and disappeared.

'Now the other one,' the Doctor hissed. And in two seconds the gallant assistant was nowhere to be seen. Juan Hagapoco, the fat matador, was left alone in the ring with five rampaging bulls.

The rest of the show was really well worth seeing. First, all five bulls went raging round the ring, butting at the fence with their horns, pawing up the sand, hunting for something to kill. Then each one in turn would pretend to catch sight of the Doctor for the first time and, giving a bellow of rage, would lower his wicked-looking horns and shoot like an arrow across the ring as though he meant to toss him to the sky.

It was really frightfully exciting. And even I, who knew it was all arranged beforehand, held my breath in terror for the Doctor's life when I saw how near they came to sticking him. But just at the last moment, when the horns' points were two inches from the sky-blue waistcoat, the Doctor would spring nimbly to one side and the great brutes would go thundering harmlessly by, missing him by no more than a hair.

Then all five of them went for him together, completely surrounding him, slashing at him with their horns and bellowing with fury. How he escaped alive I don't know. For several minutes his round figure could hardly be seen at all in that scrimmage of tossing heads, stamping hoofs and waving tails. It was, as Polynesia had prophesied, the greatest bullfight ever seen.

One woman in the crowd got quite hysterical and screamed up to Don Enrique, 'Stop the fight! Stop the fight! He is too brave a man to be killed. This is the most wonderful matador in the world. Let him live! Stop the fight!'

But presently the Doctor was seen to break loose from the mob of animals that surrounded him. Then catching each of them by the horns, one after another, he would give their heads a sudden twist and throw them down flat on the sand. The great fellows acted their parts extremely well. I have never seen trained animals in a circus do better. They lay there panting on the ground where the Doctor threw them as if they were exhausted and completely beaten.

Then with a final bow to the ladies, John Dolittle took a cigar from his pocket, lit it, and strolled out of the ring.

13. We Depart in a Hurry

As soon as the door closed behind the Doctor, the most tremendous noise I have ever heard broke out. Some of the men appeared to be angry (friends of Pepito's, I suppose), but the ladies called and called to have the Doctor come back into the ring.

When at length he did so, the women seemed to go entirely mad over him. They blew kisses to him. They called him a darling. Then they started taking off their flowers, their rings, their necklaces and their brooches, and threw them down at his feet. You never saw anything like it - a perfect shower of jewellery and roses.

But the Doctor just smiled up at them,

bowed once more, and backed out.

'Now, Tommy,' said Polynesia, 'this is where you go down and gather up all those trinkets and we'll sell 'em. That's what the big matadors do: leave the jewellery on the ground and their assistants collect it for them. We might as well lay in a good supply of money while we've got the chance – you never know when you may need it when you're travelling with the Doctor. Never mind the roses – you can leave them – but don't leave any rings. And when you've finished, go and get your three thousand pesetas out of Don Ricky-ticky. Chee-Chee and I will meet you outside and we'll pawn the gewgaws at that shop opposite the bed maker's. Run along – and not a word to the Doctor, remember.'

Outside the Bullring, Chee-Chee and Polynesia found the crowd still in a great state of excitement. Violent arguments were going on everywhere. I joined them with my pockets bulging in all directions, and we made our way slowly through the dense crowd to that side of the building where the matadors' dressing room was. The Doctor was waiting at the door for us.

'Good work, Doctor!' said Polynesia, flying on

to his shoulder. 'Great work! But listen, I smell danger. I think you had better get back to the ship now as quickly and quietly as you can. Put your overcoat on over that silly suit. I don't like the looks of this crowd. More than half of them are furious because you've won. Don Ricky-ticky must now stop the bullfighting – and you know how they love it. What I'm afraid of is that some of these matadors who are just mad with jealousy may start some dirty work. I think this would be a good time for us to get away.'

'You're probably right, Polynesia,' said the Doctor. 'You usually are. The crowd does seem to be a bit restless. I'll slip down to the ship with Chee-Chee and we'll wait for you there. You come by some different way. But don't be long about it. Hurry!'

As soon as the Doctor had departed, I found Don Enrique and said, 'Honourable Sir, you owe me three thousand pesetas.'

Without a word, but looking cross-eyed with annoyance, Don Enrique paid his bet.

Polynesia and I next set out to buy the food we needed, and on the way we hired a cab and took it along with us.

Not very far away we found a big grocer's shop which seemed to sell everything to eat. We went in and bought the finest lot of food you ever saw in your life.

As a matter of fact, Polynesia had been right about the danger we were in. The news of our victory must have spread like lightning through the whole town. For as we came out of the shop and loaded the cab up with our stores, we saw various little knots of angry men hunting around the streets, waving sticks and shouting, 'The Englishmen! Where are those accursed Englishmen who stopped the bullfighting? Hang them from a lamppost! Throw them in the sea! The Englishmen! We want the Englishmen!'

After that we didn't waste any time, you may be sure. I explained to the Spanish cab-driver, in signs, that he was to drive down to the harbour as fast as he knew how and keep his mouth shut the whole way, or the Doctor would choke the life out of him. Then I jumped into the cab on top of the food, slammed the door, pulled down the blinds, and away we went.

'We won't get a chance to pawn the jewellery now,' said Polynesia, as we bumped over the cobbly streets. 'But never mind – it may come in handy later on. And, anyway, we've got two thousand five hundred pesetas left out of the bet. Don't give the cabby more than two pesetas fifty, Tommy. That's the right fare, I know.'

Well, we reached the harbour all right and we were mighty glad to find the Doctor had sent Chee-Chee back with the rowing boat to wait for us at the landing wall.

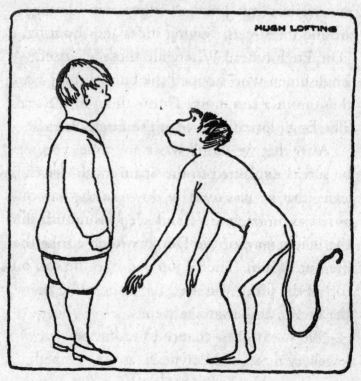

HUGH LOFTING

Unfortunately, just as we finished loading the supplies from the cab into the boat, the angry mob of Spaniards was coming onto the wharf. When they made a rush for us, Chee-Chee clambered into the boat with the last of the stores. I jumped in after him, and then we pushed off, rowing like mad for the ship.

The mob upon the wall howled with rage, shook their fists, and hurled stones and all manner of things after us. Poor old Chee-Chee got hit on the head with a bottle. But as he had a very strong head it only raised a small bump, while the bottle smashed into a thousand pieces.

When we reached the ship's side, the Doctor had the anchor drawn up and the sails set and everything in readiness to get away. Looking back we saw boats coming out from the harbour wall after us, filled with angry, shouting men. So we didn't bother to unload our rowing boat but just tied it on to the ship's stern with a rope and jumped aboard.

It took only a moment more to swing the ship round into the wind, and soon we were speeding out of the harbour on our way back to England.

'Ha!' sighed Polynesia, as we all flopped down on the deck to take a rest and get our breath. 'That wasn't a bad adventure - quite reminds me of my old seafaring days when I sailed with the smugglers. Golly, that was the life! Never mind your head, Chee-Chee. It will be all right when the Doctor's looked at it. Think what we got out of the scrap: a boatload of ship's stores, pockets full of jewellery, and thousands of pesetas. Not bad, you know - not bad.'

'What a story we've got to tell the others when we get home,' I said. 'Let's hope Dab-Dab has a nice fire burning in the kitchen.'

'Oh, I'm sure she will,' said Doctor Dolittle.

And we all laughed as the sails billowed and our little ship headed home for Puddleby-on-the-Marsh.